D0399447

SMURF CAKE

by Peyo

Ready-to-Read

Simon Spotlight
New York London Toronto Sydney New Delhi

SIMON SPOTLIGHT
An imprint of Simon & Schuster Children's Publishing Division
1230 Avenue of the Americas, New York, New York 10020

Originally published in French as *Le Gâteau Des Schtroumpfs* written by Peyo.

For information about special discounts for bulk purchases, please contact Simon & Schuster Special Sales at
1-866-506-1949 or business@simonandschuster.com.
Manufactured in the United States of America 0513 LAK
First Edition
2 4 6 8 10 9 7 5 3 1
ISBN 978-1-4424-8492-4 (pbk)
ISBN 978-1-4424-8493-1 (hc)

Papa Smurf was taking a walk when suddenly he heard his name called. “Papa Smurf, it’s an emergency!” called Cook Smurf.

“What’s wrong, Cook Smurf?” asked Papa. “I’m baking a cake for the Smurfs, and I’ve run out of eggs!” cried Cook Smurf. “I need just one more egg to finish the cake!

"Don't worry," said Papa.
"We'll smurf up an egg for you!"
Papa knew just what to do.

“Cook Smurf has run out of eggs,” Papa told Smiley Smurf and Grouchy Smurf. “Please be good Smurfs and go to Farmer Brown’s place to get an egg. We paid him for six eggs last month, but we only collected five.
So just bring one egg back!”

“I hate eggs!” replied Grouchy.
“Of course we will help!” said Smiley.
“Watch out for the chickens,”
Papa warned as the two Smurfs set off.
“I hate chickens,” grumbled Grouchy.

Farmer Brown's farm was a few miles beyond the big Smurf Forest.

“Let’s hurry up,” suggested Smiley as he jumped over a large tree branch. “I hate to hurry!” replied Grouchy.

When they reached the edge of the forest, Smiley stopped suddenly.
"Listen!" he said excitedly.
"I hear chickens clucking!"

But Grouchy was not excited.
"I hate clucking!" he complained.

Grouchy and Smiley hid in a bush
and peeked out. They saw one hen . . .
. . . and then another!
They saw little yellow chicks too.
But no eggs.
"I hate chicks!" exclaimed Grouchy.

“The eggs must be in the henhouse,” whispered Smiley.
“Let’s go, but be very careful,” he continued. “Chickens do not like to give up their eggs!”

Carefully the two Smurfs made their way toward the henhouse. . . .

But a big mother hen saw them!
"*Squawk!*" cried the hen.
"Run!" yelled Smiley.

Grouchy and Smiley ran to safety.
But they had to find another way
to smurf an egg.
Smiley had an idea.
"We can dig a tunnel!"

"I hate digging!" muttered Grouchy.
"Oh, don't be such a grouch!"
said Smiley.

After lots of digging, the Smurfs finally made it into the henhouse. “There are the eggs!” cried Smiley. “We’ll pick one out and smurf it back to the village.”

But the egg was heavy, and the little Smurfs couldn't move fast while carrying it.
Luckily, Smiley had another great idea. . . .

The big mother hen noticed something
moving toward the door.
She almost couldn't believe her eyes
when she saw that it was an egg
with a string tied around it.

Slowly the egg traveled across
the henhouse and out the door.

The big mother hen was so surprised
that she did not even squawk!
The hen chased after her egg.
At the other end of the string,
Smiley and Grouchy saw the hen
coming their way.

“Run!” cried Smiley. “The hen has smurfed us! We have to get out of here!”

“I hate hens!” said Grouchy.

But he listened to Smiley and ran!

Once they were far enough away from the henhouse, Smiley and Grouchy slowed down.
They gently carried the egg back to Smurf Village.

Finally Smiley and Grouchy proudly presented the egg to Papa Smurf. "Good work!" said Papa Smurf. "Now Cook Smurf can finish baking our Smurf cake!"

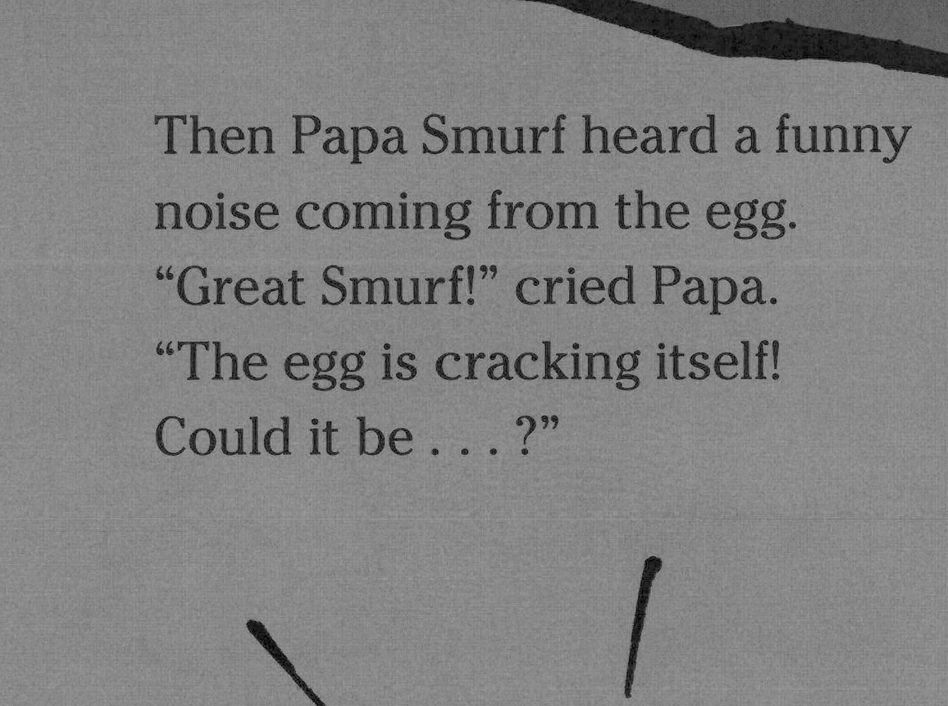

Then Papa Smurf heard a funny
noise coming from the egg.
"Great Smurf!" cried Papa.
"The egg is cracking itself!
Could it be . . . ?"

Yes, it could be!
As Papa and Smiley watched in surprise, a little yellow chick hatched out of the egg!

The little chick had a piece of its shell on its head, making it look like the chick was wearing a funny hat. "Cook Smurf definitely can't use that egg!" exclaimed Papa.

“I know just what to do,” said Papa.
“I will give Cook Smurf my book of magic recipes so he can bake a Smurf cake without the egg!
It will be the best cake ever!”

“I hate cakes!” complained Grouchy.
But the little chick seemed to
like Papa’s idea very much!

Thanks to the magic recipe book, Cook Smurf baked the most delicious cake ever—and he didn't even need the egg! All the Smurfs were so happy that Papa threw a party to celebrate. But one Smurf did not join the fun. "I hate parties!" grumbled Grouchy.